# FLYING FERGUS

## The Secret
## Cycle Scoop

First published in Great Britain in 2018 by
Piccadilly Press
80-81 Wimpole Street, London, W1G 9RE
www.piccadillypress.co.uk

Text and illustrations copyright © Sir Chris Hoy, 2018

This is a work of fiction. Names, places, events and incidents are either the
products of the author's imagination or are used fictitiously. Any resemblance to
actual persons, living or dead, or actual events, is purely coincidental.

A CIP catalogue record for this book is available from the British Library.

ISBN: 978–1–848–12640–4
also available as an ebook

1 3 5 7 9 10 8 6 4 2

# FLYING FERGUS

## The Secret Cycle Scoop

# CHRIS HOY

## with Joanna Nadin

Illustrations by Clare Elsom

Piccadilly
PRESS

# Meet Fergus
## and his friends. . .

Fergus

Chimp

Grandpa Herc

Daisy

Jambo Patterson

Mum

Mikey McLeod

Minnie McLeod

Wesley Wallace

Calamity Coogan

Dermot Eggs

Sorcha

Charlie Campbell

Choppy Wallace

Belinda Bruce

. . .and see where they live

Fergus's house

Daisy's house

NAPIER STREET

Herc's Hand-Me-Downs

Bandstand

Play park

CARNOUSTIE COMMON

Bruce's Biscuits

# Meet Princess Lily
## and her friends...

**Hector Hamilton**

**Princess Lily**

**Unlucky Luke**

**Percy the Pretty Useless**

**Demelza**

**Douglas**

Dimmock

King Woebegot

Prince Waldorf

Queen Woebegot

Duke Dastardly

Prince Derek

Knights of No Nonsense

Scary Mary

# Two Lots of Trouble

Fergus Hamilton was an ordinary nine-year-old boy. He liked footballs (but not when Dermot Eggs kicked them at his head), tennis balls (but not when his dog Chimp chewed them so much they went soggy and sticky and covered his hand in spit), and meatballs (but not if his mum's fiancé Jambo was there for tea because he always snuck them off Fergus's plate when he wasn't looking!). He didn't like card games (because he always lost), board games (because he always got bored), or games lessons at school when they had to use the balance beam (because he couldn't stay on one foot and always fell over).

Yes, he was ordinary in almost every way, except one. Because, for a small boy, Fergus Hamilton had an extraordinarily big imagination.

Some days he imagined a world in which, instead of planning an enormous wedding, his mum and Jambo were planning a secret ceremony safari adventure (although he wasn't sure Mum's white dress would look so great covered in jungle mud).

Some days he imagined a world in which, instead of maths and history, you could learn to do bike tricks like alley-oops and bunny hops and manuals all day (although he was pretty sure Minnie would ace all the tests, whereas he'd get a B and a lot of bruises).

And some days he imagined a world in which, instead of cats and dogs, you could have amazing mythical creatures like unicorns and hippogriffs for pets (although he was pretty sure Chimp wouldn't take too kindly at sharing his bed with a hippogriff.)

But this particular morning Fergus was imagining a world in which, instead of being in a massive grump, his best friend Daisy was her usual fact-spouting, joke-making, bike-loving brilliotic self.

He just didn't understand what was wrong with her. When Daisy had missed out on getting into the starting line-up for the Internationals, Fergus had been upset too. But since then she'd been working really hard to prove herself as first reserve. With Mikey down with glandular fever, Calamity off visiting his gran, and Dermot fiddling with his phone most of the time, she didn't have that much competition for the slot anyway.

It could be his new second best friend Sorcha, he supposed. Daisy hadn't been too keen on her at first – after all, Sorcha and her sister had beaten them in the Wreck-It Run. But she and Sorcha seemed to be great mates now, and Daisy had learned more sign language than even he had, so the pair of them chatted away with their fingers, leaving Fergus floundering and asking, "What does *that* mean?" every few minutes.

No, there was something else on her mind, and something big.

And she wasn't the only one.

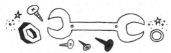

Jambo picked up that evening's copy of the *Carnoustie Courier*, read the back page, then slapped it back on the table with a sigh.

"Another one?" asked Fergus's mum.

"Aye," replied Jambo.

"Another what?" asked Fergus, who had been so busy worrying about Daisy, he'd missed most of what was going on at home in the last day or so.

"Another leaked story about us lot," said Grandpa Herc, with a grim look. "At this rate, every team in the world will know all of our tactics before we even get to Manchester."

A flustered Fergus snatched up the paper, turned to the headline sports story and began to read.

CARNOUSTIE COURIER

# SPORT

# SWEET DREAMS OF SUCCESS

**Report by Dickie Moore**

The Courier's sports supremo Dickie Moore can exclusively reveal that Hercules' Hopefuls are using more than pedal power in their bid to take the top spot at next month's Internationals. According to our secret source, they'll be taking their own pillows with them to make sure they get a good night's sleep ahead of each race. And that's not all. Our mole will have loads more of the team's top tips and sneaky cheats for you over the next few days, so that you can see what gives these hopefuls – or should we say "sure-fire winners"? – the edge, on the track, and off it.

"What a lot of rot!" declared Grandpa.

"Too right!" agreed Fergus. "I mean, the pillow thing's true, thanks to Choppy. And I reckon it's a dancer of an idea. But the story makes it sound like we're cheating!"

"And who's the Phantom Leaker?" demanded Grandpa. "That's what I'd like to know."

"Me too," said Jambo. "Because my boss reckons if I don't come up with a scoop to rival Dickie Moore in the next week, then I might as well clear my desk."

Fergus felt himself flush with anger for a second time. "But you're the best sports reporter in the city, and the *Evening News* is the best paper."

"Not any more," said Jambo with a sigh.

"Och, love." Mum gave him a hug. But not even that could put a smile on Jambo's face.

"I'm worried, Jeanie," he said. "With the wedding coming up, I really can't afford to lose my job."

"And you won't," she insisted.

"No, you won't," said Fergus, adding his support, as well as a hug of his own. "We'll get to the bottom of it. Me and Daisy. You'll see."

Now all he had to do was persuade his best friend. Fergus knew that if this had been a few weeks ago she'd have been the one leading the investigation, with a list of suspects already drawn up, as well as tactics to take them down.

But with the way Daisy had been acting lately, Fergus was worried he'd struggle to even get her on board.

## Disappearing Daisy

Fergus burst into the changing rooms at Middlebank to find the air already buzzing with talk of the Phantom Leaker.

"I reckon it's Mikey," announced Belinda. "He's probably phoning the *Courier* from his sick bed this minute!"

"Don't be daft," snapped Mikey's sister, Minnie. "He's not been to practice in a week, so how would he even *know* any secrets?"

"You might be passing them on," Wesley pointed out. "Maybe you're in on it too. Maybe *you're* selling secrets for money!"

"I'm not, and nor is Mikey," said Minnie, folding her arms in a huff.

"Minnie's right," added Fergus. "He may be off ill, but Mikey's a team player through and through. He'd never do that to us."

"Well, what about Calamity then?" demanded Wesley. "Or *you*, even." He pointed accusingly at Fergus.

Fergus felt himself bristle. "Now you really are talking rubbish," he said. "Why would I do that to my own team? Or to Jambo? You know he might lose his job over this."

"Really?" asked Minnie, softening now.

Fergus nodded. "His boss is worried

Dickie Moore at the *Courier*'s scooping him on every story."

"What's scooping?" asked Wesley.

"Yeah, scooping?" repeated Dermot, looking up from his phone for the first time all morning.

"It means getting a big story first," explained Fergus. "And either he has to come up with one, or we need to stop the Phantom Leaker handing over any more details to that sneak Dickie Moore."

"So why don't we just tell Jambo our real tactics?" demanded Wesley. "He gets a scoop, problem solved."

"I think looping round that track too fast has sent your head into a spin," boomed a voice behind them.

Fergus turned to see Wesley's dad, Choppy Wallace, standing in the doorway with his hands on his hips and a dark look on his face.

"No it hasn't," said Wesley, his own face reddening.

"Well, you don't seem to be thinking straight, son," said Choppy. "We don't want *anyone* to know our tactics, that's the whole point. Not the Brisbane Belters, not the Lyon Licketysplits and especially not the Shanghai Shooting Stars."

"Oh, right," admitted Wesley. "Of course."

"So what *do* we do?" demanded Belinda.

"We do what we do best," said another voice.

Fergus grinned as Grandpa Herc walked into the room. "What's that?" he asked.

"We get racing, of course," said Grandpa, smiling.

"But what about the Phantom Leaker?" asked Wesley.

Grandpa raised one bushy eyebrow. "Well, we just have to hope that whoever it is has heard enough this morning to make them stop."

Fergus frowned. He couldn't believe it. It was almost funny when Wesley had accused them but now Grandpa seemed to think one of them really was the Leaker. Worst of all, Grandpa was hardly ever wrong which would mean . . . the Leaker was in this room right now! He scanned his friends' faces, trying to work out who it might be. Definitely not Minnie, she was too loyal. And not Belinda – her dad owned Bruce's Biscuits, and she had a pony, a parakeet and a swimming pool, so she definitely didn't need the money. Could it be Calamity? Fergus didn't think so.

He might trip over his legs on a regular basis, but he never said the wrong thing. That left Wesley and Dermot. Dermot never came up with any ideas of his own, and lately he'd been more interested in playing on his new phone to notice what was even going on anyway.

So maybe it *was* Wesley. He'd been the first one to accuse Mikey, but that could be to cover his own guilt. And he had a history of tricks behind him, after all. Most of them against Fergus.

As the team set out onto the track, Fergus stared at the back of Wesley's head, imagining he could see inside, and find out what he was up to. But all he could make out was the number one emblazoned on his helmet.

"Hang on a minute," Grandpa called out from the front of the pack. "Where's Daisy?"

Fergus felt his heart jump. How could he have forgotten Daisy? They'd only just made up and he was messing up already. And Grandpa was right, where *was* she? She was never late to practice.

But then a horrible thought crept into his head and his stomach dropped.

She wouldn't.

She couldn't.

No. Of course she absolutely couldn't and wouldn't. Daisy would NEVER do anything to harm the Hopefuls.

Only . . .

"Well, that's solved it," said Wesley. "The Phantom Leaker must be Daisy. She's selling secrets because she's still in a sulk."

"I wouldn't be surprised," added Choppy. "We all saw what a bad loser she was when she lost out on a spot on the team."

"No," said Fergus quickly. "Not Daisy." But even as he said it, he couldn't be sure he was right. It *was* all a bit odd – her moods, and now her disappearance.

"Haven't we had enough of guessing games?" said Minnie. "No one knows the truth. Not yet."

"Aye," agreed Grandpa. "And we've work to do, with or without Daisy. So let's get on."

But out on the track, the squad were all over the place, their heads too full of the Phantom Leaker to concentrate on any of the new tactics Choppy and Grandpa had been trying out.

"I look forward to seeing this shambles on the back page of the *Courier* tomorrow," grumbled Grandpa. "I can see the headline now – 'Hercules Hopeless' or something snide like that."

"Don't blame us," said Wesley, angrily. "Blame Daisy."

"It's not Daisy's fault you couldn't take those turns today," said Grandpa. "*That* kerfuffle was all down to you, sonny."

"Whatever," mumbled Wesley.

But as he cycled home, Chimp trotting behind, Fergus tried to push away a horrible feeling that Wesley might be right this time.

"I don't understand it," Fergus said to Mum as she looked through a brochure for expensive-looking flowers. "Daisy's just disappeared. She won't even come to the phone when I call."

"I wish I could help, Fergie," said Mum. "But you know what Mrs D's like. She'll not tell me anything. Remember when Daisy was off nursery and we were guessing she had the plague by the end of it because Mrs D wouldn't say?"

Fergus nodded. "And it was only chicken pox." Then he had a thought. "Maybe she's ill now," he added. "Maybe she really can't come to the phone."

"Maybe," said Mum.

"She hasn't been to the hospital, has she?" Fergus blurted, his head suddenly bursting with horrible thoughts of accidents or deadly diseases.

Mum shook her head. "Fergie, I don't know anything. I don't think Daisy's ill, and I don't think she's the Phantom Leaker either. But I do think something big must be bothering her."

Fergus nodded. "Aye," he replied. "I just wish I knew what."

## The Phantom Leaker
## Strikes Again

When the *Courier* dropped onto the doormat that evening, and Chimp trotted into the kitchen with it in his mouth, Fergus could hardly bring himself to take it off his dog.

"It won't bite," said Jambo, looking up from the stew he was stirring. "The paper, I mean."

"I'm not so sure," said Fergus. But he took the newspaper from Chimp.

Chimp wagged his tail, waiting for a pat for helping, or maybe something tasty from the kitchen counter, but Fergus barely noticed his faithful friend. He turned straight to the back page, heart pounding faster than it did after a four-lap sprint. When he saw the headline, he let out a gasp.

"No way!"

"What?" demanded Jambo, his spoon stuck mid-air, dripping sauce on the floor, much to Chimp's delight. "What is it?"

## SPORT

# Deserter Daisy Proves She's Not Top Team Material

**Report by Dickie Moore**

"No way!" said Jambo when Fergus read the headline out.

"Yes way!" said Fergus. "Listen to this: 'Hercules Hopefuls' first reserve Daisy Devlin failed to show up for team practice today, and rumour has it she's been in a cycling strop for weeks over her low ranking.'"

"Och, no," said Mum.

25

"There's more," said Fergus. "'According to our mole, Devlin risks being dropped from the squad altogether if she doesn't buck up her ideas.'" Fergus shook his head in disbelief. "That's not even true. Grandpa would never do that."

"Choppy might," said Jambo.

"Do you think *he's* the Phantom Leaker?" asked Fergus.

"Och, Fergie. I don't know my own ankle from my elbow right now. But I do know one thing. I'm in big trouble with the big boss at the office tomorrow. Another scoop for the *Courier* – even if it's not true – means I'll be for the high jump."

Fergus gulped. "There must be *something* we can do."

Mum nodded. "*Anything*, Jambo?"

But Jambo shook his head, looking miserable. "Short of asking Dickie to name his source – which he'll never do – I can't think of a single thing."

Fergus felt himself brim with anger. This wasn't fair and it wasn't right. Jambo had done nothing wrong at all, and nor had the team, and they were the ones suffering. And all the while the Phantom Leaker – whoever it was – was probably laughing at them.

"Can I go out?" Fergus said suddenly.

"Where to?" asked Mum.

"Sorcha's," said Fergus decidedly. Because Sorcha was the only friend he had who wasn't tied up in the team. And the only friend he had aside from Daisy who was clever enough to work any of it out.

Mum frowned. "Well, tea's nearly ready, isn't it, Jambo?"

Jambo looked at the stew and shrugged. "This'll keep," he said. "I've lost my appetite anyway."

"Och, go on then," said Mum. "But only an hour, mind."

Fergus nodded. "Come on, boy!" he called to Chimp, and the pair shot swiftly out of the door, down the stairs, and round the corner to Sorcha's house.

Sorcha was having trouble writing words down fast enough for Fergus to read them, and Fergus found himself making another silent promise to learn more sign language. *If only Daisy was here*, he thought. But then, wasn't that half the problem? He took the pad from Sorcha.

At least you know it's not Daisy now.

Why would she sell stories that made her look bad?

"I suppose," signed Fergus, feeling his spirits lift a little. But only a little.

"So who?" he signed.

Sorcha took the pad again.

*I hate to ask, but could it be Jambo?*

*He does need money for the wedding, he said so himself.*

Fergus thought for a moment. Mum had been looking at a lot of fancy wedding things recently. Maybe Jambo felt he had to get extra cash on the side . . .

But no sooner than he'd thought it, he shook it off.

"No way," he signed back, then took the pad.

His job at the Evening News is on the line if the leaks don't stop.

And anyway, we might not be well off, but Jambo'd never do it to the team.

And nor would my mum, before you suggest that too!

Sorcha looked indignant and took the pad.

I wasn't going to!

"Sorry," Fergus signed.

"Me too," signed Sorcha back. Then she wrote,

I wish I could be more help.

"We need Daisy," Fergus said out loud, signing it too.

"Three heads are better than two," signed Sorcha.

Fergus wrote on the pad,

But Daisy won't talk to me.

Sorcha thought for a moment, then, grinning, snatched the pad.

*So we make her!*

"How?" asked Fergus. "I've tried everything."

Sorcha smiled so wide Fergus thought her face might crack.

> You've tried everything you can think of.
>
> But you haven't tried the famous Sorcha Henderson Sit-In.

"The Sorcha Henderson Sit-In?"

"Aye," signed Sorcha. "It never fails."

Fergus felt his spirits lift again, higher this time, and he let out a small laugh – the first one in days. Because, for the first time in days, he felt like he might, actually, be getting somewhere.

# The Sorcha Henderson Sit-In

"So how does this work?" Fergus asked Sorcha as the pair settled down on Daisy's doorstep the next morning, with Chimp at their feet.

Sorcha passed Fergus the pad.

It's a sit-in, we just sit!

"Fair enough!" Fergus signed, and laughed.

But the longer they sat, the less amusing it all seemed to be. And the less Fergus felt like laughing. Because inside his head, dark thoughts swirled like inky fog:

*What was up with Daisy?*
*Would she come to the door?*
*Who was the Phantom Leaker?*
*Would Jambo lose his job?*
*What was Chimp chewing right now?*
*Hang on . . .*

"Chimp!" he hissed.

Chimp looked up, an enormous flower like a giant dandelion clock hanging out of his mouth.

"Drop that!" urged Fergus. "If Mrs Devlin sees you, she'll have your tail for a duster."

"What's going on?" signed Sorcha.

"Chimp." He pointed, and Sorcha grinned. But Fergus shook his head and wrote on the pad.

> *If Mrs D catches us, she'll have a conniption fit!*

"What's that?" asked Sorcha.

"I don't know," signed Fergus. "And I don't want to. Daisy says they're worse than Choppy Wallace on a bad day."

> *Crikey!*

wrote Sorcha, who had been told a lot about Choppy and Wesley, and the old rivalry between the two teams.

> *Exactly.*

Fergus wrote, then passed the pad to Sorcha.

This time, Sorcha paused.

"What is it?" signed Fergus.

A wide smile spread over Sorcha's face again.

But don't we WANT Mrs Devlin to hear us?

We need to get her attention.

Then she'll HAVE to meet our demands!

Fergus was puzzled.

What demands?

Sorcha pressed so hard the pencil nearly snapped.

To see Daisy!

Or had you forgotten?

Fergus shook his head. "Sorry," he signed. "My head's in a bit of a spin. But you're right. Let's do it!"

And with that, Fergus, Sorcha and Chimp set about making as much kerfuffle as they could possibly muster.

First they tap danced.

Then they drummed on the doorstep with some sticks.

Then they jumped up and down as many times as they could in a row (117 for Sorcha and 109 for Fergus).

Then they threw an apple into the bushes for Chimp to fetch. But, despite the hoohah Chimp made fetching it, not even a curtain twitched.

Then Fergus had a brainwave. "Oh no!" he yelled. "Don't do that, Chimp!"

"Do what?" signed Sorcha.

Fergus winked, and wrote as he shouted.

*Don't wee on the roses!*

Sorcha giggled.

"No!" yelled Fergus and Sorcha together. "Don't do it!"

Sorcha wailed with laughter.

"Really," continued Fergus. "Don't WEE ALL OVER MRS D'S PRIZE ROSEBUSH!"

That was all it took. In two seconds

flat the front door was open, framing a fuming Mrs Devlin.

"Fergus Horatio Hamilton, what *do* you think you're playing at?" she demanded. Then she spotted Sorcha. "And Sorcha Henderson, I thought better of you."

"She can't hear you," said Fergus.

Mrs Devlin blushed at her mistake.

Sorcha wrote on the pad and held it up so Mrs D could see.

But I'm getting better at lip-reading every day!

Daisy's mum ignored it. "That dog had better not have done any funny business in my front garden," she said. "And what are you doing dawdling on my doorstep on a damp morning, and without coats? You'll catch a chill and that could turn into pneumonia and then, well, you might be rushed off to hospital and have to stay there for months, years even."

"Maybe you should let us in before

that happens?" suggested Fergus. "We only want to see Daisy for a minute."

Mrs Devlin's lips went very thin, which they always did when she was cross, or worried, which was nearly all of the time. But then she said. "Och, maybe *you'll* be able to talk some sense into her. Heaven knows, I've tried hard enough, but she'll not listen to her own mother."

So something big really *was* up – it had to be for Mrs Devlin to give in so easily. Daisy's house was usually a fortress, with Mrs D guarding the gates like a giant, fanged hound.

"We'll do our best," he promised, as she held the door open for the friends.

"But not with muddy paws!" said Mrs Devlin sharply, as Chimp trotted in. "Pick him up, quick!"

Fergus smiled to himself as he picked Chimp up to carry him up the stairs. She was still the same old Mrs D.

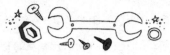

"Keep Out!" read the sign on Daisy's bedroom door. But Sorcha wasn't about to obey that, and knocked hard three times.

Nothing.

So she knocked again, and this time Fergus joined in. "Let us in, Daisy!" he demanded. "What's going on?"

"Nothing," came the eventual answer, as full of gloom as a rainy Sunday.

Fergus flinched. Clearly that was a lie, and demanding she talk to them wasn't going to work. He looked at Sorcha, who shrugged. Then he had an idea.

"Dais, we need your help. Something terrible's happened to the team."

Fergus crossed his fingers and wished very hard, and saw Sorcha do the same.

Silence.

Then he heard a creak and a shuffle, then a click as the door slowly opened.

"Daisy?" Fergus asked, almost checking it was her, because she didn't look like her usual bouncy self. Even her curls seemed less springy.

But that wasn't all.

Daisy's bedroom walls had always been covered in posters – some of Spokes Sullivan wheeling down the back straight, some of bike bits and general knowledge, and some straight out of the newspaper of Hercules' Hopefuls themselves. But now the walls were completely bare. If Fergus had been worried before, now he was really terrified.

"Daisy?" he asked again. "What's going on?"

But Daisy didn't answer. Instead she just stood aside to let them in, then sat back down on the bed, dejected. "Go on then," she said. "What's so terrible?"

Fergus took a big breath. "Someone's leaking secrets about the team to the *Courier*," he said. "Which means Jambo's set to lose his job, and we're set to lose the Internationals as everyone will know our tactics."

"Who would do that?" asked Daisy, less dejected now and more surprised. "Wesley?"

"No one knows," admitted Fergus. "Wesley thought . . . he thought it might be you. Only because you've been in such a grump and then you didn't show up at all," he said quickly, waiting for his best friend to explode angrily.

"Me?" said Daisy. But then she shook her head and instead of looking cross, she just looked sad. "Och, whatever, it doesn't matter anyway."

Fergus felt his legs wobble with worry. What *was* going on with Daisy?

Sorcha must have read his mind at that moment. "Now it's your turn to tell us what's going on," she signed to Daisy, then took the pad.

> And don't say 'nothing' because we're your friends and we know that's not true.

Daisy's eyes began to brim with tears.

"Och, Dais," said Fergus. "What is it? Are you injured? Are you ill? Are you scared about the Internationals? Is that it?"

Daisy snorted. "As if!" she snapped. "I'm not scared of anything!" Then she sniffed. "Well, maybe something."

"What?" signed Sorcha.

Daisy looked up. "Dad's got a new job in Inverness," she said.

"But that's . . . miles away," said Fergus. "How will he drive there every day?"

Daisy wrote on the pad as she spoke so Sorcha could see.

> It's a hundred and fifty-six miles.
>
> But he won't be driving.

"Flying, then?" tried Fergus. "Blimey, what a palava."

"He won't be flying, either."

Sorcha was looking at Daisy with a strange expression on her face.

"But how will he get to work then?" Fergus went on, confused. "Teleport? Only I don't think they've invented that yet." *At least, not in this world,* he added to himself.

Sorcha and Daisy looked at each

other and grimaced. Then Daisy looked even sadder than before.

"Think," Sorcha signed patiently to Fergus.

Fergus thought. And thought. And then, with a slow seep, realization came to him like cold water.

"Och, no way, Dais," he said.

"Yes," said Daisy, a sob welling in her throat. "Yes way. Fergie. . . we're moving."

"When?" asked Sorcha.

Fergus crossed his fingers hoping his friend was going to say in six months, or even a year.

"That's the worst bit," said Daisy. "At the end of this week! No more school. No more practice. And definitely –"

"No Internationals," interrupted Fergus, as the awful truth dawned on him. "But you can't! You can't just . . . *go*. Once a Hopeful, always a Hopeful!"

"Not any more," said Daisy. "I don't know who I am any more. But hopeful? Ha! I'll never be hopeful again."

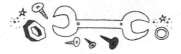

Fergus shut Daisy's front door behind him. He had told the girls that Chimp really did need a wee this time, but it wasn't that. He needed to think, and think hard. Was Daisy really going to leave? She'd been his best friend since he was a bairn, and they always spent all day at school together. She'd been his number two on the team since Grandpa set it up. She couldn't just go. He'd be left on his own. Well, with his other team-mates and Chimp and Sorcha, but none of them were *Daisy*. The only person who came close was . . .

"Chimp," he said, "get your helmet on. We've got some flying to do."

And without a backwards glance, Fergus slid into his saddle, scooped Chimp into his lap, and set off towards the park as fast as he could. Once, twice, three times he back-pedalled and then FLASH! . . .

# Dragon Danger

Fergus soared through the sky at speed. He'd never been more desperate to see his friend Lily. It occurred to him that he could visit Nevermore – a parallel universe – whenever he wanted, but Inverness, which was in the same country, seemed an impossible distance to travel. And with that thought in his head, he landed in Nevermore with an even heavier *WHOMP* than usual, right in the middle of the racetrack.

Or what was supposed to be the racetrack. Only this one seemed to have turned into some kind of dragon farm.

"Lawks a mussy!" came the shriek. "Get orf the track!"

It was Queen Woebegot. Fergus shot her a worried glance, waiting for her to change her mind and demand "orf with their heads" instead.

"No worries, Sheila!" Chimp replied. "We're getting orf – I mean off. Come on, mate," he added then to Fergus, who was mesmerised by Demelza the dragon breathing fire all over the slalom poles.

Fergus snapped out of it, sped to the sidelines with Chimp alongside him, and slipped out of the saddle. They hopped over the barrier into the stands where Hector Hamilton, Fergus's dad and coach for the Palace Pedallers, was sitting.

"I was worried you weren't going to make it," said Hector.

"Make what?" asked Fergus.

"Dragon Danger Zone?" suggested Chimp. "Death Valley?"

"About that," added Fergus worriedly. "What are they doing here? I thought they'd been cleared out? Has something happened? Is racing . . . banned again?"

Hector grinned. "Not at all. Welcome to the Dragon Derby," he explained. "And Douglas and Demelza are only pets, they're not dangerous at all. Not that the queen would agree."

"I'm not sure *I* agree," said Fergus, who had just seen Douglas land on the back straight, making a divot as deep as a ditch.

"Make it stop!" the queen shouted, though to whom it wasn't clear. "It's far too dangerous. Everyone will perish!"

"No, we won't, Mum," came a voice from the starting line. "We'll all be just dandy."

Fergus felt himself heave with relief at the sight of Princess Lily pulling on her helmet. She was still here, and still safe. He waved and she waved back, giving him the thumbs up and nudging her teammates Unlucky Luke, Scary Mary and even her brother, the cantankerous Prince Waldorf, to do the same.

"You'll be better than dandy," Fergus called over to them. "Win this one and you've won the championship!"

"Yes, best of three, remember," added his dad loudly. "And you're one up already, Pedallers."

"Not if we have anything to do with it," sneered Prince Derek from the starting line, where he was snapping on his own all-black helmet and adjusting his all-black kit. Beside him, the other Darklands Demons – Nigel, Norris and Norman – did the same. "Come on, girls," he called then.

Chimp shot his head up. "Girls?" he asked. "But . . . "

Fergus followed Derek's eyeline and felt his throat tighten. "I don't think he was talking to his team," he managed to squeak out.

"Who then?" asked Chimp.

"Th– th– them," stammered Fergus, pointing a shaking finger at a gleaming black horsebox, out of which descended two more dragons. These beasts didn't look anything like the palace pets. Instead of being a cheery green, and having clipped toenails, these dragons were the colour of crows and sported enormous claws and sharpened fangs.

"Meet Beryl and Gladys," announced Derek.

"Orf with their heads!" shrieked the queen, somewhat predictably.

"Oh," said Duke Dastardly, uttering his first words of the afternoon. "You didn't think it was fair to just use *your* little dragons, did you?"

"He has a point," admitted King Woebegot.

"Orf with *your* head," snapped the queen at her husband.

But the king didn't even flinch. He had been threatened with head-orfing several times a day for ten years and barely even heard it any more.

Fergus and his dad did, though, as well as Beryl's terrible roar. "I'm not sure," Hector said to the king. "I really don't think —"

"Objection overruled," barked King Woebegot. "Come along, everyone. Let's get this started. Cook's making my favourite for lunch and I'm getting awfully peckish."

"You're not the only one, mate," said Chimp, eyeing Beryl, who in turn was eyeing Unlucky Luke a little hungrily.

As the riders lined up for the starting whistle, Fergus felt shaky for the second time that day. Losing Daisy to a house move was one thing, but she'd still only be 156 miles away. Losing Lily to a dragon . . . He tried to push the horrible thought from his mind. "Stay focused on the good stuff," he heard a voice inside his head say. Wasn't that what Grandpa was always telling him?

"They'll be just dandy," came another voice. But this voice was definitely Dad. "The team have been practicing hard, they're ready for it."

"Thanks, Dad."

"Don't worry, Fergus. Everyone just needs to do their best," Hector said.

Fergus nodded. He would do his best. Just like he knew Lily and the gang would. He still felt a bit worried about those dragons, though.

"On your marks . . . " came the call.

Fergus crossed his fingers.

"Get set . . . "

Chimp crossed his paws.

"Go!"

The pair of them crossed their hearts, closed their eyes, and hoped that dragons were vegetarian after all.

# Who Needs
# a Handsome Prince?

"Great going, Lily! Keep your eyes on the prize!"

Fergus heard his dad's praise, but he still couldn't face watching. He'd opened his eyes once or twice, but every time he looked one of the dragons seemed to be dangerously close to swiping a rider with their tail so that they tumbled off, or coughing smoke in their path so that they crashed into a barrier. He knew from the noise that Norman and Waldorf had already come a cropper. That left just six cyclists in all, and one lap still to go.

"They're only going to pull it off!" Fergus's dad nudged him. "Lily's riding a blinder today. You've really got to see this, son."

Fergus steeled himself. His dad was right. What sort of an assistant coach

was he if he couldn't face the race – even if there were a few dragons? He opened his right eye, then the left, and saw the glory for himself. There was Lily, blazing down the back straight, with Unlucky Luke and Scary Mary not far behind, all of them managing to weave in and out of the wandering dragons. And way ahead of Derek, Nigel and Norris!

But that's when it happened.

First Douglas trod on Gladys's toe, so that Gladys let out a mighty bellow, scaring Beryl, who roared in rage and clattered into Demelza, who started a stampede right across the track.

Scary Mary screamed and swerved. Unlucky Luke braked so hard, the straps snapped on his special pedals and he flew over his handlebars. Then Lily, who had managed to stay on course, found herself caught up and corralled with the dragons into the corner. Seizing their advantage, Derek, Nigel and Norris swept past and on to victory.

"Och, no!" wailed Fergus's dad.

"That's a downer and a half, mate," agreed Chimp.

But Fergus didn't care about the race. He cared about Lily, who was stuck in the corner, surrounded by very cross dragons. Pets or no pets, they were all enormous, they could all breathe fire, and two of them could do some serious damage with their teeth and toenails.

"My daughter! Do something!" shouted King Woebegot to the Knights of No Nonsense, who had been standing idly by, discussing the state of the flower beds.

"Yes, orf with everyone's heads!" commanded the queen.

"I don't think that will be necessary," said Duke Dastardly calmly. "Yet. Derek?"

"I've got this," answered Derek, a touch smug, and pulled what looked like a long, green, flashing pole from a sheath attached to his bike frame.

"What's that?" demanded Waldorf.

"Oh, only a Dragon-Defence 3000 Stun-Sword," drawled Derek.

"You had that all along?" demanded Unlucky Luke. "Cheater!"

"Hardly," said Derek. "Check the rules if you don't believe me."

Fergus knew Derek was right. His dad hadn't put anything in the rules forbidding weapons, because he hadn't known Stun-Swords would be needed, or even existed.

"Stand back," said Derek then, aiming his Stun-Sword at Demelza, who was the closest to Lily.

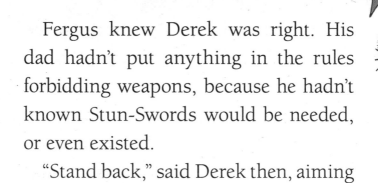

"Are you sure that won't hurt?" asked Waldorf. "She's a very . . . sensitive dragon."

"She doesn't look that sensitive to me," said Chimp, eyeing the massive beast.

"Oh, it'll just sting a bit, then she'll sleep for a week." Derek hovered his finger above a red button.

"Stop!" screamed the queen. "You'll hit my Lily."

"Exactly, stop!" added Lily, finally finding her voice. "Who said I wanted *his* help anyway?"

"Oh, every princess needs a handsome prince to rescue them." The duke smiled.

"Not *this* princess," snapped Lily. "And besides, I can't see a handsome prince." She pretended to survey the track.

"Thanks a lot," protested Waldorf.

"Nope," said Lily. "No handsome princes. All I need right now is a friend. Fergus?"

Hearing his name, Fergus snapped to attention, his fear suddenly slipping somewhere deep inside. "I'm coming," he called. "Don't move!" And he jumped over the barrier, Chimp springing behind him.

"Oh, and what are *you* going to do? Read them a poem?" demanded the duke nastily. "Do a little dance?"

"Actually," said Lily, "that's the best idea you've had all day. Possibly ever." And she nodded at Fergus, who nodded back, suddenly realising exactly what Lily wanted.

After all, the dragons were no scarier than Mrs Devlin. Not really. "Yoo-hoo!" Fergus yelled, waving his arms about and dancing a reel. "Look over here!"

The dragons looked. So did everyone else.

"That's right!" he called. "You don't want Chimp to do a wee on the flowerbeds, do you?"

"Steady on, mate," said Chimp. "We're in company."

"Just follow my lead," hissed Fergus, and began to boogie across the track.

Chimp followed, wiggling his own Waltzing Matilda in time to a tune in his head.

Fascinated, the dragons followed too. First Douglas, then Demelza, then Beryl and Gladys, who seemed to be swinging their hips along with Chimp.

"That's it," urged Fergus.

"Good dragons," added Lily, managing to mount her bike again, even giving Gladys a pat on the backside as she passed.

"You're good to go!" shouted Fergus.

Lily didn't need telling twice. Pushing down hard on the pedals, she sped down the final straight to cross the finish line.

"Race is over," snapped Derek, sulking that he hadn't got to use his Stun-Sword.

"But not the championships," Lily

pointed out. "And now we're even. And besides, I feel like I won anyway."

"How?" demanded Derek. "Because you look like you're standing in last place to me, little girl."

"Little girl, is it?" Lily scoffed. "Well, this little girl just proved she doesn't need a Stun-Sword or a handsome prince. Not now and not ever. I can rescue myself, thank you very much."

Fergus coughed.

Lily laughed. "With a little help from my friends."

"See you soon, son," said Dad as the gang gathered to say their goodbyes after a slap-up lunch at the palace.

"Aye," agreed Fergus. "Last race of the championship. I wouldn't miss it for the world."

"Sure you can't hang around?" asked Lily. "We could go swimming tomorrow if you did. In the Lake of Swords."

"Rather you than me, mate," said Chimp, shuddering.

Fergus smiled. "I wish I could. But you know I can't."

"I know," said Lily. "And I know something else. Doesn't matter how long you're gone, or how far away you are, you've always got a friend in me."

"And me," said Unlucky Luke.

Waldorf pulled a face but Lily nudged him. "And me," he admitted.

As Fergus climbed back on his bicycle, his heart felt fuller than it had in days. He would always have Lily.

And, no matter how far away she was, he was pretty sure he'd always have Daisy too. With a little help from her, and Sorcha, he'd find out who the Phantom Leaker was and fix things for Jambo and Mum so the wedding could go ahead.

Well, actually he might need more than a *little* help this time, because right now he was out of ideas. But he was determined, and as Grandpa – and Dad – were always saying, that's halfway to winning already.

## Daisy's Deception

"What took you so long?" asked Daisy, as Fergus and Chimp blustered back into the bedroom.

Sorcha wrote on the pad.

Chimp been drinking puddles again?

"Or getting chased by cats again?"

Fergus smiled. "Och, just the odd dragon or two," he said.

Daisy rolled her eyes. "Well, while you've been having a laugh in La-la-land, or wherever it is you disappear off to in your head, back here in the real world we've come up with a plan."

And it's BRILLIOTIC!

Sorcha wrote, using her new favourite word.

"You're seriously suggesting we make up fake tactics, tell them to a team member, and then hope they show up in the paper?" said Fergus, once the girls had explained their scheme.

"Aye," said Daisy, Sorcha nodding along with her. "That way we catch the crook, and no one's the wiser about what we're up to. Well – what *you're* up to," she corrected herself.

"'We'," Fergus corrected back. "It'll always be 'we'."

Daisy shrugged, her face falling again. "Maybe," she said. Then Fergus saw her jaw set as she gathered herself. "But if we don't do this there might not be a team to be part of, I can tell you that for nothing."

"So what do we try out first?" asked Fergus.

Sorcha waved the pad at Fergus.

Heated knickers!

"You have got to be joking." Fergus shook his head. "Who'd believe we were using heated knickers?"

"We'll say they keep our bum muscles warm before the race," said Daisy. "That's important, keeping muscles at the right temperature. Even you know that." She raised a cheeky eyebrow.

"Ha-ha," replied Fergus. "But really? Knickers?"

Sorcha and Daisy looked at each other, then back at Fergus, big grins on their faces. "Knickers!" they signed.

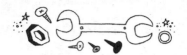

The knickers story was the easy part, it turned out. The three friends had taken ages to decide who to tell the story to.

Daisy was all for starting with Wesley. "He's been difficult before," she pointed out. "And his only loyalty is to himself."

"Aye." Fergus had to agree. "But he was so angry about it. You didn't see him, Dais. I don't think Wesley's that good an actor."

"So who then?" asked Sorcha.

"Mikey?" Daisy suggested.

"Still in quarantine," replied Fergus.

"Belinda?" tried Sorcha.

"Still rich," said Fergus. "Why would she need to sell stories? Besides, her dad has got shares in the *Evening News* so she's hardly likely to sell stories to the *Courier* and put her dad's paper out of business – then they'd have no money."

"Fair point," agreed Daisy.

Fergus thought and thought. They'd already ruled out Minnie and Calamity on loyalty grounds. They just knew none of the original Hopefuls could be behind the leaks. Choppy was a suspect, but he was off buying stock for his shop so they'd have to wait until tomorrow to try him. There was no way it could be Grandpa. Then Fergus remembered something. "Dermot!" he blurted.

"What, Dermot the Dimwit?" asked Sorcha.

Fergus nodded. "He's been so busy on his new phone I assumed he wasn't really interested in tactics at all. But what if he's been earwigging all along and instead of playing games he's been texting secrets straight to Dickie Moore?"

"He *was* taking an awful lot of photos on his phone up at the track last week," added Daisy.

"So we start with him then," said Fergus.

"Makes sense," signed Sorcha.

"Do you want to tell him or shall I?" asked Daisy.

Fergus felt himself shudder at the thought of discussing heated knickers with anyone, let alone Dermot. But, he had faced those dragons. "I'll go," he said. "You've got packing to do," he added, his heart sinking a little at the thought.

But Sorcha had other ideas. "No," she signed. "Daisy has to do it." She switched to her pad, writing quickly.

He already thinks Daisy's in a mood with everyone, so he'll believe she'd snitch on Choppy's new idea before he's told the rest of us.

Daisy nodded. "I'm not ready to pack yet," she said. "It feels too . . . final. And this might be the last chance I get to help the team. And, what's more, I owe you. I owe everyone."

Fergus smiled. "No, *we* owe *you*," he said. "We doubted you, and all along you were in trouble."

Tears threatened to spill down Daisy's cheeks again.

Sorcha quickly wrote,

No time for that now.

You've got work to do.

"And no buts," added Fergus. "Because
. . ." he prompted.

Daisy brushed the tears away, then
allowed herself the smallest of smiles.
"Butts are for sitting on," she finished.

So with that, the threesome and Chimp set off down the stairs, past an astonished Mrs Devlin, and straight down the road to Dermot's house.

While Daisy disappeared into Dermot's, Fergus, Sorcha and Chimp found themselves sitting on a doorstep for the second time that day – this one belonging to Julie Gilhoolie, the lollipop lady. "Well, you can hardly sit on Dermot's doorstep!" Daisy had pointed out.

And there they stayed until, fifteen minutes later, Daisy hurried round the corner to join them.

"Did you do it?" asked Sorcha.

Daisy nodded.

"And do you think he believed you?" asked Fergus.

Daisy nodded again. "He was typing on his phone the whole time I was telling him," she said. "And he even took a photo of me. Though Dickie Moore had better not put that in the paper."

"*If* it's him," pointed out Sorcha. "Dermot, I mean. We don't know for sure, after all."

"Aye," agreed Fergus. "*If.*"

But as the four of them walked slowly home, Fergus had a funny feeling that they were right.

The funny feeling stayed with him all through lunch, as he and Grandpa munched marmalade sandwiches, and all through the afternoon, as he and Chimp played footie on Carnoustie Common, right up until the moment when the letterbox rattled, and that evening's copy of the *Courier* dropped *PLOP!* onto the doormat.

## Hold the Back Page!

"Hot Pants A-Go-Go for Hercules' Hopefuls!" screamed the headline.

Then, underneath, the lies continued.

Fergus felt his stomach flip at the same time as his mouth slipped into a smile. Because those were Daisy's exact words – the ones they'd agreed she would tell Dermot and swear him to secrecy.

Well, the secret was out now, that was for sure.

# SPORT

# HOT PANTS A-GO-GO FOR HERCULES' HOPEFULS

**Report by Dickie Moore**

Hold on to your hats – or should we say pants? – because you're not going to believe the latest twist to team tactics over at Hopefuls' HQ! According to our mole, the desperate pedallers are turning to heated knickers to help win the race, believing these special pants won't just warm them up quicker, but will give them the edge in next month's Internationals. 'They're clutching at straws,' our mole told us, 'What will it be next? Supersonic socks?'"

"Blimey O'Riley," said Jambo, scanning the page for a second time to make sure he'd read it right.

"Is it true?" asked Mum.

"What do you think?" asked Grandpa, shaking his head solemnly. "Heated knickers! Where do they get these ideas?"

At that, Fergus could hold it in no longer. "We did it!" he blurted. "We made it up! Daisy told Dermot and he must have fed it to Dickie. It was Dermot all along!"

"No way," said Jambo.

"Yes way," replied Fergus.

"Och, Fergie. You lied to the paper?" said Mum.

Fergus felt his elation deflate. "Well . . . I . . . "

"Hang on, Jeanie," Grandpa said, saving Fergus from his struggle to find words. "The boy's played a blinder. He didn't lie to the paper. He set a trap for Dermot, that's all. He's outed the Phantom Leaker, and given Jambo here the scoop he's been waiting for!"

Jambo's face lit up as he realised what was staring right at him in black and white. "Herc's hit the nail on the head, Jeanie. This is the story of the century! Well, of tomorrow's sports pages anyway. I'm phoning the boss now to tell him to hold the back page."

"Hang on," Fergus said. Because he'd thought of something then. The hard pip at the heart of all this hoo-hah. "Don't name Dermot," he pleaded.

"Why ever not?" asked Jambo. "He didn't do you any favours, after all. He put the team in danger."

"I just . . . I don't think he meant to be mean," Fergus said. "I think . . . I think something else is going on."

Mum nodded. "Good boy, Fergie," she said. "You and Grandpa need to get to the bottom of it before anyone starts naming names."

"We will," Fergus promised. "Won't we?" He turned to Grandpa.

"Sure as eggs is eggs," Grandpa replied.

"Dermot Eggs." Fergus smiled, thinking of his team-mate's last name. But the smile slipped no sooner than it had started. Solving the story had been one thing, but maybe there was a bigger story behind it. A badder story.

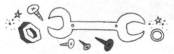

"It wasn't me," repeated Dermot for the fifth time. "It was . . . Chimp!" He pointed at the dog in desperation, having already accused half of the squad.

"Och, Dermot," said Grandpa. "We know you did it. Daisy here only told you about heated knickers so you'd leak it to Dickie Moore. No one else knew about that silly story."

Daisy nodded in agreement. "As if we'd use heated knickers," she added.

"As if we could afford heated knickers," Fergus added.

As he realised his defeat, Dermot's face crumpled. "I'm sorry," he sobbed. "I didn't mean to make things worse. I only did it —"

"Yes, why *did* you do it?" interrupted Daisy, still miffed.

"Let the laddie finish," said Grandpa softly.

Fergus felt sadness soak his own thoughts as he saw Dermot wipe his face on his sleeve.

"I . . . I needed the money," he said.

"You can see where I live."

Fergus found himself checking the shelves and noticing how little there was on them. And when Dermot had offered them a drink, the fridge had been almost empty too.

"How can I keep up with Wesley?" continued Dermot. "My Swift's getting rusty and I haven't got half the kit. No wonder I'm last reserve."

"Hey," Grandpa warned. "The reason you're last reserve is nothing to do with your kit. That's down to commitment – or lack of it."

"And some things are more important than money," said Daisy. "Like honesty!"

Dermot reddened.

Fergus's face fell. Daisy was right, and so was Grandpa. But now Dermot had admitted it, they needed to move on. They could moan about him, or they could do something to help him.

Mum had taught Fergus that. "But that's not to say we don't understand," he said to Dermot then. "Look at me. I didn't even have a bike when I started out."

"Nor me," admitted Daisy. "Fergus and Herc helped me mend an old one."

"Really?" asked Dermot.

"Really," said Fergus. "And if you want, I'm pretty sure we can do something for you. Can't we?" He turned to Grandpa, hope written all over his face.

Grandpa's frown slowly fell. "Aye, sonny," he said finally. "I reckon we can. Nothing is ever so broken it can't be fixed."

Fergus thought of his best friend, and all the worries they'd had, and the worries to come now she was moving. But, like Grandpa also said, where there's a will, there's a way. And Fergus was always willing.

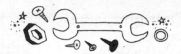

"I'm not doing everything for you," Fergus said, as he handed Dermot the oil can. "I'm just showing you how to take better care of your bike so it doesn't matter that it's not brand new."

Dermot took the can and smiled. "Your grandpa's already done enough," he said. "Herc got all the rust off for me, and your mum mended my old jersey." He turned to show off the invisible stitching, which of course, they couldn't see.

"And you can have this too," said Daisy holding something out to him. "I . . . I won't be needing it any more."

"Your Hopefuls water bottle?" Fergus asked. "But –"

"No buts . . . " said Daisy.

"Butts are for sitting on!" finished Dermot.

Fergus felt happier than he had since the whole Phantom Leaker episode began as he, Daisy and Dermot worked on the bike together that afternoon.

Happier still when Jambo held up the *Evening News* outing Dickie Moore for being pranked – a picture of Fergus and Daisy grinning out from the back page, taken by Dermot himself.

But as Fergus slipped under his Spokes Sullivan duvet that night, the loss of Daisy washed over him again, and the sorry sight of her handing over her precious team water bottle pricked tears in his own eyes. How were the Hopefuls going to win the Internationals without her?

How was *he* going to do *anything* without her?

No, he thought to himself, clutching Chimp for comfort (a little too tightly for Chimp's liking), things were never going to be the same again.

## Once a Hopeful,
## Always a Hopeful

"Och, Fergie, for the fifty billionth time, will you get out into the sunshine?" Mum flapped a magazine at Fergus as he lay morose on the sofa.

"Aye," agreed Jambo. "You look like you've lost a pound and found a penny. Go on, it's a dazzler of a day out there. Why not go for a quick spin – say, over to Daisy's?"

"What for?" Fergus asked glumly.

"It won't change anything. Daisy's still going to be gone tomorrow."

"All the more reason to make the most of today then, I'd say." Mum raised an eyebrow at Fergus.

He knew he was defeated. Sighing, he hauled himself up and trudged to the door.

Chimp leapt to his feet and wagged his tail at the prospect of a walk.

"Well, at least someone's found their inner winner," said Grandpa. "He's been as blue as you since you both woke up."

Fergus glanced down at his dog. It was true that Chimp seemed to absorb his own sorrow somehow.

"Go on," said Grandpa. "Take Chimp for his walk. And remember, if it's hard for you, it's a hundred times worse for Daisy."

Fergus felt his cheeks redden. Grandpa was right. How could he have been so selfish? He needed to make it up to Daisy, and fast. "Have I got any pocket money owing?" he asked Mum.

"Only this week's," she replied. "And what's in your piggy bank."

"Oh." Fergus's big idea balloon went pop as he remembered he only had twenty pence left after buying Chimp chews.

"But you can write me an IOU," offered Grandpa. "If this is for what I think it is."

Fergus puffed with purpose again. "It is," he said. "At least, I think it is."

"Come on then, sonny, let's stop at the shop before you get off."

Fergus almost felt his own tail wag as he and Chimp trotted down the stairs to Grandpa's stockroom to pick out the present he had in mind.

"Here," Fergus said, handing the hastily wrapped parcel over, as he and Daisy sat amongst bubble wrap and towers of packing boxes in the Devlins' front room.

"What's this then?" Daisy asked.

"Open it!" Fergus told her. "You'll need it where you're going. Believe me."

Daisy carefully peeled back a flap of wrapping paper, before thinking better and tearing into it, excited at what might be inside. But when she saw the present, her face fell and she slumped back against a stack of suitcases. "A Hopefuls' water bottle?" she said, incredulous. "What do I want with that now?"

Fergus felt himself slump too. But only for a second. *If it's hard for you, it's a hundred times worse for Daisy*, he heard Grandpa tell him. "Because you should be proud of where you come from," Fergus said. "Because you'll *always* be a Hopeful, no matter where you live."

Daisy's lips flickered into the beginning of a smile.

Fergus saw, and carried on. He was going to make this day a good one, however bad he felt inside. "Because whatever squad you join in Inverness – and you had better join one – they should know what you're made of," he said. "That you were on the team that won the Nationals. And the team that's going to the Internationals in . . . " he paused as he worked it out, ". . . three weeks' time! Crikey."

Daisy grinned. "No," she said. "Better than that. The team that's going to *win* the Internationals in three weeks' time!"

Fergus felt a flutter of something wonderful in his heart. "You think?" he asked.

"I know," replied Daisy.

At that, Fergus hugged his friend before she could see him cry.

"Och, give over,' she said, sensing it anyway. "I'll be back for the wedding, now that's all back on."

"Promise?" he asked.

"Promise," she replied. "I'm a bridesmaid, after all. Can't let your mum down on her big day."

"Or me. I don't want to be the only one in a ridiculous outfit!"

"Exactly," agreed Daisy. "So I'll be back before you know it."

"I should go," Fergus said then. "Jambo's making pancakes for tea and they go horribly soggy if you're late."

Daisy pulled a face.

"I don't suppose . . . " Fergus tried then.

"I'll get my bike," said Daisy. "And tell Mum," she added. "She'll probably think I'm going to be poisoned if I eat pancakes for tea. They're for breakfast only in this house."

For once, Mrs Devlin didn't even argue, just waved them away with a roll of packing tape, so Daisy and Fergus cycled side by side back to the flat, chatting tactics and talking teamwork, before clattering up the stairs and settling down at the table for their pancake feast.

"We'll miss you, Daisy," said Mum, "but you know you'll always have a place at our table."

"Aye," agreed Jambo.

"To Daredevil Daisy!" said Grandpa, raising his glass of ginger beer in honour. "Fearless and fast."

"To Daredevil Daisy," everyone agreed.

Daisy's face reddened at the attention and for a moment Fergus thought she might even cry, but then, she raised her own brand-new water bottle, and clinked it against Fergus's glass for good measure. "Once a Hopeful, always a Hopeful," she said.

At that, Fergus felt his heart grow so big it might actually burst through his shirt.

"Always," he agreed. "And forever."

**Joanna Nadin** is an award-winning author of more than seventy books for children, including the bestselling Rachel Riley diaries, the Penny Dreadful series, and *Joe All Alone*, now an acclaimed TV series. She studied drama and politics at university in Hull and London, and has worked as a lifeguard, a newsreader and even a special adviser to the Prime Minister. She now teaches writing and lives in Bath, where she rides her rickety bicycle, but she never, ever back-pedals...

www.joannanadin.com

**Clare Elsom** is an illustrator of lots of lovely children's books, including Maisie Mae and the Spies in Disguise series. She is also the author-illustrator of Horace and Harriet. Clare studied Illustration at Falmouth

University (lots of drawing) and Children's Literature at Roehampton University (lots of writing). Clare lives in Devon, where she can be found doodling, tap dancing and drinking cinnamon lattes.

www.elsomillustration.co.uk

**Sir Chris Hoy MBE,** won his first Olympic gold medal in Athens 2004. Four years later in Beijing he became the first Briton since 1908 to win three gold medals in a single Olympic Games. In 2012, Chris won two gold medals at his home Olympics in London, becoming Britain's most successful Olympian with six gold medals and one silver. Sir Chris also won eleven World titles and two Commonwealth Games gold medals. In December 2008, Chris was voted BBC Sports Personality of the Year, and he received a Knighthood in the 2009 New Year Honours List. Sir Chris retired as a professional competitive cyclist in early 2013; he still rides almost daily. He lives in Manchester with his family.

**www.chrishoy.com**

# FLYING FERGUS

The moment the squad
has been waiting for is here -
the International Championships!

Find out what happens to Fergus and friends
as they face the Brisbane Belters and
the Shanghai Shooting Stars . . .

Catch up with Fergus and friends
in their new adventure

## The Photo Finish

### COMING SOON